SURPRISE, ANGELICA!

Based on the TV series *Rugrats*® created by Arlene Klasky, Gabor Csupo, and
Paul Germain as seen on Nickelodeon®

SIMON SPOTLIGHT
An imprint of Simon & Schuster Children's Publishing Division
1230 Avenue of the Americas
New York, New York 10020

Manufactured in the United States of America
First Edition   4 6 8 10 9 7 5

Library of Congress Cataloging-in-Publication Data
Gold, Becky.
Surprise, Angelica! / by Becky Gold ; illustrated by Vince Giarrano.
p.   cm. — (Ready-to-read. Level 2)
Summary: Angelica tries to scare Chuckie and the other Rugrats, so that she can
be the first to see Susie's gerbils.
ISBN: 0-689-82829-2 (pbk.)
[1. Babies—Fiction.   2. Gerbils—Fiction.   3. Behavior—Fiction.]
I. Giarrano, Vince, ill.   II. Title.   III. Series.
PZ7.G5434Su   2000
[E] dc21
99-16405
CIP

SURPRISE, ANGELICA!

by Becky Gold

illustrated by Vince Giarrano

Ready-to-Read

Simon Spotlight/Nickelodeon

"Get it, Spike!" Tommy called to his dog. He threw a ball in the air. Spike caught it. "Good boy!"

"Catching a ball is nothing," said Angelica. "Susie's new gerbils play *inside* balls."

"What are germ balls?" Tommy asked.

"Not germ balls, *gerbils*," Angelica replied. "They're a kind of rat who live in dark caves. And Susie has invited me over to see them."

"That sounds scary, Angelica!" exclaimed Chuckie.

Just then Tommy's mom, Didi, called them in. "Susie's here," she said.

"Can we see Susie's gerbils, too?" Tommy asked Angelica.

"You babies stay here," Angelica warned. "Gerbils are very dangerous. They have sharp teeth that can chew through anything—high chairs . . . 'frigegators . . . everything!"

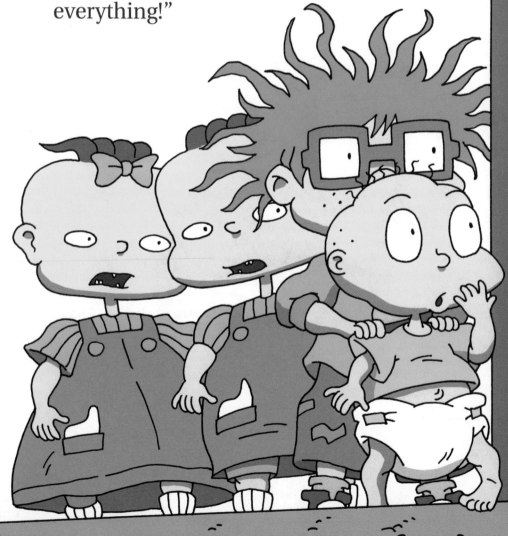

"Everything?" Chuckie gasped.

"That's right, Finster," Angelica said.

She wanted to be the first to see the gerbils.

"Hey, you two are shivering like Jell-O," Susie said when she saw the babies. "What's the matter?"

"Susie, aren't you afraid to live with cave rats?" Chuckie asked.

"Yeah," said Tommy, "'specially ones with shark teeth?"

"You mean the gerbils? Why don't you come over to meet them?"

Tommy and Chuckie shook their heads. Susie stared at Angelica. She had a feeling she knew why they weren't coming over.

"So, Susie," said Angelica, "ready to go?"

"Tell you what," Susie said, "I'll go home first and prepare the gerbils for your visit. They don't like surprises. I'll come get you when they're ready."

"Oh, okay," Angelica said.

"Why she gots to repair them, Angelica?" asked Tommy.

"Yeah," Phil said. "Maybe they're broke."

"Maybe they gots too many germs!" Chuckie exclaimed.

"She said *prepare*, not repair, you dumb babies!" said Angelica.

When Susie got home, she told her brother Edwin how Angelica had scared Tommy, Chuckie, Phil, and Lil.

"Well, Suse," Edwin replied, "maybe Angelica just needs a taste of her own medicine. Come on, I'll help you."

After a while, Angelica started getting antsy. Those gerbils must be prepared enough, she thought. She went next door and rang the bell. Susie answered.

"I was just coming to get you," said Susie, huffing and puffing.

"Why are you breathing funny?" Angelica asked.

"I was running to get the gerbils more things to chew," Susie explained, "They're teething like crazy!"

"What's that?" asked Angelica. She pointed to the floor. It was covered with big, gray spots.

"Gerbil tracks," Susie said.

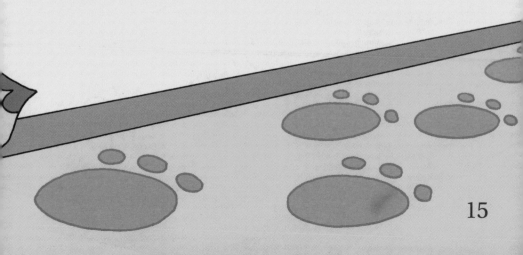

"Uh . . . is that their food?" asked Angelica.

"Just a snack for later," Susie replied. "This is Frankenrat's bowl . . . and this is Igor's," she said, pointing. "And these are boxes for them to chew on."

"Susie," said Angelica, "maybe the gerbils need to chew some more. Maybe they aren't ready to meet me yet. Maybe . . . we should go play outside!"

"No," Susie said. "They've been waiting for you! Follow me!" She led Angelica upstairs.

Suddenly they heard a loud growl, followed by angry snarls. Angelica didn't know that Edwin was behind the door making the noises. She ran back down the stairs.

19

The doorbell rang again. It was Tommy, Chuckie, Phil, and Lil.

"Hi, gang!" Susie said.

"We were afraid," Tommy told her, "but a baby gots to be brave."

"So you're all ready to meet the gerbils?" Susie asked.

"YEAH!" cried Tommy, Phil, and Lil.

"N-n-no," said Chuckie.

"Hey, where's Angelica?" Tommy wondered.

"I don't know," said Susie. "She was here a minute ago."

"Who made the big poker dots?" asked Phil.

"Edwin did," Susie answered. "Come on upstairs."

"Oh, no," Chuckie mumbled. "I don't want to go up there!"

"Oooooooh!" exclaimed Lil.

"They don't look like rats," said Phil.

"And this doesn't look like a cave," added Lil.

"Gerbils aren't rats," said
Susie. "Angelica was just
scaring you."
She gave them the gerbils
to hold.

"Gerbils are fuzzy," said Tommy.
"They don't bite," added Chuckie.
"And they don't growl," said Edwin. "But they *do* like to chew—on cardboard!"

Everyone took a turn at holding the gerbils.

"I need names for my gerbils," Susie told them. "Any ideas?"

"How about Frankenrat? Or Igor?" a voice said.

It was Angelica.

"You tricked me," she told Susie. "That was mean!"

"Well, you played a mean trick to keep the babies away!"

"Okay, okay," Edwin said. "Time to let bygones be bygones."

"Huh?" the babies said at once.

"Edwin's right," Susie said. She smiled and held out a gerbil. "Do you want to hold her?" she asked Angelica.

Angelica took the gerbil, which nuzzled her hand.

"Let's put them in their rockin' rollers," said Susie.

The babies chased the gerbils all over the floor.

Then they watched them chew pieces of cardboard into tiny bits.

"Hey, this one runs fast," said Tommy.
"Can we call it Zoomer?"

"Sure, Tommy," Susie agreed. "And
because this one tickles, I'll call it Tickles!"

"Zoomer and Tickles, the bestest gerbils
in the world!" said Tommy.

Look for these

Ready-to-Read Books

LEVEL 3

READY-TO-READ

A Children's Book-of-the-Month Club Main Selection

Susie wants to show the babies her new pet gerbils, but the babies are afraid of them. Are gerbils really cave rats with sharp teeth that can chew through anything, as Angelica says? Find out in this funny, easy-to-read story!

Ready-to-Read books offer children a world of possibilities at four different reading levels:

PRE-LEVEL 1 Recognizing Words

- Word repetition
- Familiar words and phrases
- Simple sentences

LEVEL 1 Starting to Read

- Simple stories
- Increased vocabulary
- Longer sentences

LEVEL 2 Reading Independently

- More-complex stories
- Varied sentence structure
- Paragraphs and short chapters

LEVEL 3 Reading Proficiently

- Rich vocabulary
- More-challenging stories
- Longer chapters

Look for other Rugrats Ready-to-Read Books at your favorite bookstore and library!

0300

NICKELODEON   KLaSKY CSUPO INC.

A Ready-to-Read Book/Fiction
SIMON SPOTLIGHT/NICKELODEON
Simon & Schuster, New York
VISIT OUR WEB SITES: www.SimonSaysKids.com and
www.nick.com

US $3.99 / $5.99 CAN

ISBN 0-689-82829-2

UPC   0 76714 00399 6   82829

TO PARENTS AND TEACHERS:

Children learn to read in a variety of ways: through formal teaching in school, by being read aloud to at home, and by reading on their own, using all the tools they've learned for making sense of letters and words. The process starts with a child's first awareness that letters on the page form words, which make sentences, which make stories. No one method of learning is right for every child, but *all* children need books they can read successfully.

Ready-to-Read books feature stories by authors who really know how to write for this age group. They're grouped at four levels:

- **Pre-Level One,** with repetitive text and simple sentences for children who can recognize words
- **Level One,** with an expanded vocabulary and longer sentences for children who are just starting to read. Some Level One books also use rebus icons to further help readers.
- **Level Two,** for those who are reading independently and are ready for slightly greater challenges
- **Level Three,** for children who can read on their own, with fewer illustrations and longer texts

At each level the books are all written, designed, and illustrated to suit the interests, needs, and abilities of new readers.

Children in preschool and the early elementary grades are universally fascinated with reading, and are already saying, "I'm ready to read." When they finish a **Ready-to-Read** book, we want them to say, "I *am* reading, and I like it!"

G.I. JOE
THE RISE OF COBRA

DUKE'S MISSION

by Michael Teitelbaum
based on the story by Michael Gordon and Stuart Beattie & Stephen Sommers
and the screenplay by Stuart Beattie and David Elliot & Paul Lovett
illustrated by Shane L. Johnson

Ready-to-Read

Simon Spotlight
New York   London   Toronto   Sydney

SIMON SPOTLIGHT
An imprint of Simon & Schuster Children's Publishing Division
1230 Avenue of the Americas, New York, New York 10020

Based on Hasbro's G.I. JOE® Characters

CHAPTER ONE

The huge weapons factory sprawled out across a large stretch of desert. Standing outside its main building were two soldiers, Captain "Duke" Hauser and Lieutenant "Ripcord" Weems.

Duke was about to lead a team of soldiers on a dangerous mission.

"All right, everybody, listen up," Duke called out. "We'll have the Cougar patrol vehicles in the front and back of the convoy. The Grizzly armored truck will travel in the middle, carrying the weapons case. Two Apache helicopters will cover us overhead. Okay, let's move!"

An unknown enemy desperately wanted the weapons, and it was Duke's job to see that the weapons were delivered safely to Ganci Air Base.

Ripcord drove the lead Cougar with Duke sitting beside him. The captain kept his eyes trained on their surroundings, as well as on the armored Grizzly behind them.

"That thing back there isn't going to explode, is it?" Ripcord asked Duke as he drove.

"The weapons haven't been activated yet," Duke replied. "Still, try not to hit any potholes."

Then he called into his radio, "Mother Goose, this is Bird Dog. We have the package and will make Ganci Air Base at oh-nine-hundred hours."

"I hate all that 'Mother Goose,' 'Bird Dog' stuff," Ripcord complained. "Why can't we just say 'Hey, Pete, it's Bill'?"

Duke sighed. "Eyes on the road, Rip," he said. Then he flipped the radio on again. "How's that radar looking back there, Cougar?"

In the Cougar at the back of the convoy, a soldier stared at his radar screen. Two green dots moved across the screen.

"All clear," the soldier reported. "All I've got on my screen are the two choppers in the sky above us."

"Good," Duke answered. "Let's keep it that way."

High above the convoy, a large, dark aircraft flew quickly and silently. It was a Typhoon gunship . . .

. . . and it was not detected on the radar screen of the Cougar.

CHAPTER TWO

Panels on both sides of the Typhoon gunship opened, and two cannons slid out. With a thunderous boom, they fired at the same time.

Energy blasts from the cannons slammed into the first Apache helicopter.

KA-THOOM!

The quiet of the desert was shattered as the chopper exploded and crashed to the ground in front of Duke and Ripcord's Cougar.

"Bird down!" Ripcord shouted, slamming on the brakes.

The Cougar screeched to a stop. Ripcord and Duke stared in shock at the fallen helicopter.

"Back up! Back up!" Duke yelled before grabbing the radio. "Mother Goose, this is Bird Dog. We are under attack! Repeat, we are under attack!"

Ripcord threw the Cougar into reverse and zoomed backward. Just then the Typhoon blasted the second chopper out of the sky.

"What is that thing?" Duke shouted.

"I don't know!" Ripcord yelled back.

The aircraft kept shooting and hit the Cougar at the back of the convoy.

"Stop!" ordered Duke.

Ripcord jammed on his brakes again.

As their vehicle stopped short, Duke and Ripcord jerked back in their seats.

"Who's in that thing?" Ripcord asked.

"I don't know," Duke replied. "But they just took out both choppers. And now they're wiping out the convoy."

"At least they haven't hit the Grizzly yet," Ripcord said. "The weapons are still safe."

THOOM! BOOM! THOOM!

Both soldiers looked through their back window in horror. The gunship had started blasting again, and this time it was aiming for the Grizzly truck that held the weapons.

CHAPTER THREE

Powerful blasts from the gunship slammed into the Grizzly. The armored truck burst into flames.

"They've hit the Grizzly!" Ripcord shouted. "Now what?"

"We get the weapons so they don't fall into the hands of these guys," Duke replied, "whoever they are."

"Right," Ripcord agreed. "Let's go!"

Duke grabbed his door handle. "We go on three. One—two—"

FOOM! Suddenly Duke felt a jolt shoot right through his whole body, and realized that his Cougar was no longer on the ground.

"We've been hit!" he yelled as their vehicle tumbled end over end through the air, completely out of control.

"Rip, are you all right?" Duke called. His head was spinning and he couldn't see straight. What's more, he got no answer from his buddy.

"Rip!" Duke shouted.

The Cougar finally came to a stop, landing upside down on its roof. Inside, Duke and Ripcord crashed onto the vehicle's ceiling.

Duke looked over at his partner, still feeling a little dazed. Seeing that Ripcord was hurt, Duke said, "Come on, I'm getting you out of here."

"Can't I stay and take a nap?" Ripcord asked weakly.

"Nap later. Run now," Duke replied before kicking open the door.

Duke pulled Ripcord from the Cougar, draping his friend over his shoulder. Then he ran as fast as he could.

Spotting a deep ditch straight ahead, Duke headed for it and jumped in with Ripcord—just as their vehicle exploded.

Duke made sure Ripcord was comfortable before telling him, "Stay here. I'll be back."

"Where are you going?" Ripcord asked.

"To get that weapons case before *they* do!" Duke said.

CHAPTER FOUR

After blasting every vehicle in the convoy, the Typhoon gunship now hovered just a few feet above the ground.

The door of the plane slid open, and the leader of the attack force jumped out. Her name was Ana. She was followed closely by six specially-trained Viper soldiers.

"I'm going after the weapons case," Ana told her team. "You take care of the soldiers."

While the Vipers battled the soldiers in Duke's convoy, Ana hurried to the Grizzly truck.

She dug through the smoking wreckage and found the weapons case.

"You're coming with me," she said, pulling the case from the truck.

"Wrong, Ana!" Duke shouted, stepping up to her. He was shocked to discover that the leader of this mission to steal the weapons was an old friend.

"Hello, Duke," Ana said calmly as she clutched the weapons case firmly.

"Hand over the case," Duke said.

"Good-bye, Duke," was all Ana said before she raced back toward the Typhoon.

CHAPTER FIVE

From out of nowhere, the G.I. JOE Howler
Transport appeared in the sky. Ropes dropped
from the aircraft.

G.I. JOE agents Snake Eyes, Scarlett, and
Heavy Duty slid down the ropes.

Who are these guys? Duke wondered. Are
they after the weapons too?

Duke got his answer quickly. The three members of G.I. JOE rushed right at the Viper soldiers.

With skilled ninja moves, Snake Eyes jumped over two Vipers, taking them down from behind and disarming them.

At the same time, Scarlett fired her crossbow pistol, knocking the weapons from the hands of two more soldiers.

Heavy Duty fired his machine gun–grenade launcher. The huge explosion sent the remaining Vipers flying.

I don't know who these guys are, Duke thought, but I'm glad they showed up.

As the G.I. JOE team battled the Vipers, Ana tried to make her escape.

"You're not getting away with that case!" Duke shouted, charging after her.

Duke was fast, but so was Ana. Every time he thought he was gaining on her she seemed to run a little faster.

Finally, just as Ana approached the Typhoon, Duke tackled her to the ground. The weapons case tumbled out of her hands, and Duke scrambled to grab it.

"It's over, Ana," Duke said. "You failed."

Suddenly a grappling line dropped from the Typhoon gunship. Ana grabbed the line. Then the aircraft lifted into the sky, taking Ana with it.

As the Typhoon disappeared from view, Duke
hurried back to where he had left Ripcord.

"Nice of you to come back for me," Ripcord said as Duke helped him out of the ditch. "Did you save the package?"

"Sure did, buddy," Duke replied.

"You're a real hero, Duke," Ripcord said with a smile.